LEGO NINJAGO

DRAGONS RI

NINJA DUELS

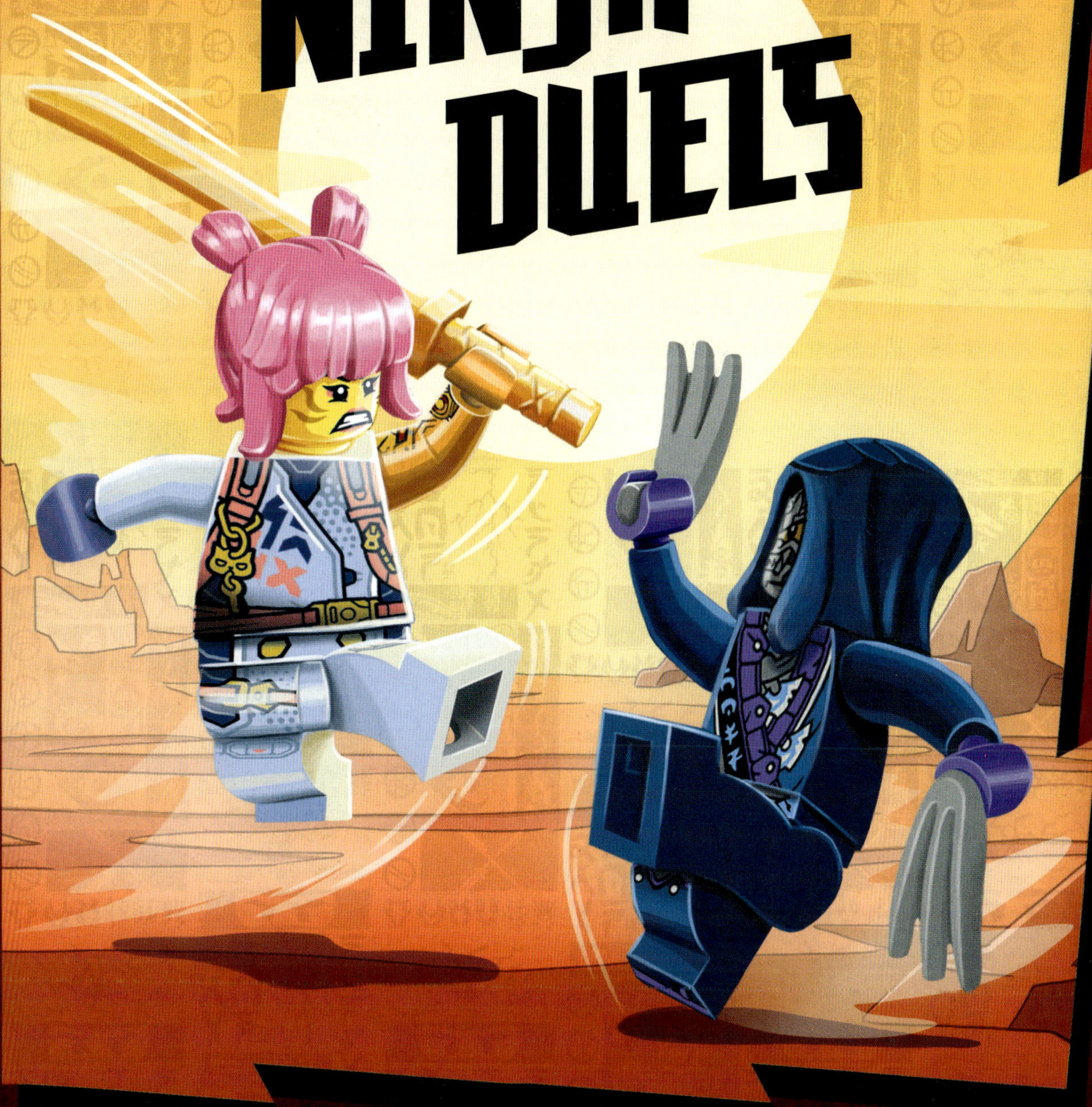

How to play

1 Remove all the parts from the box.

2 Use the instructions on pages 4–5 to build the minifigures.

3 Use the instructions on pages 6–7 to build the double-sided play scene.

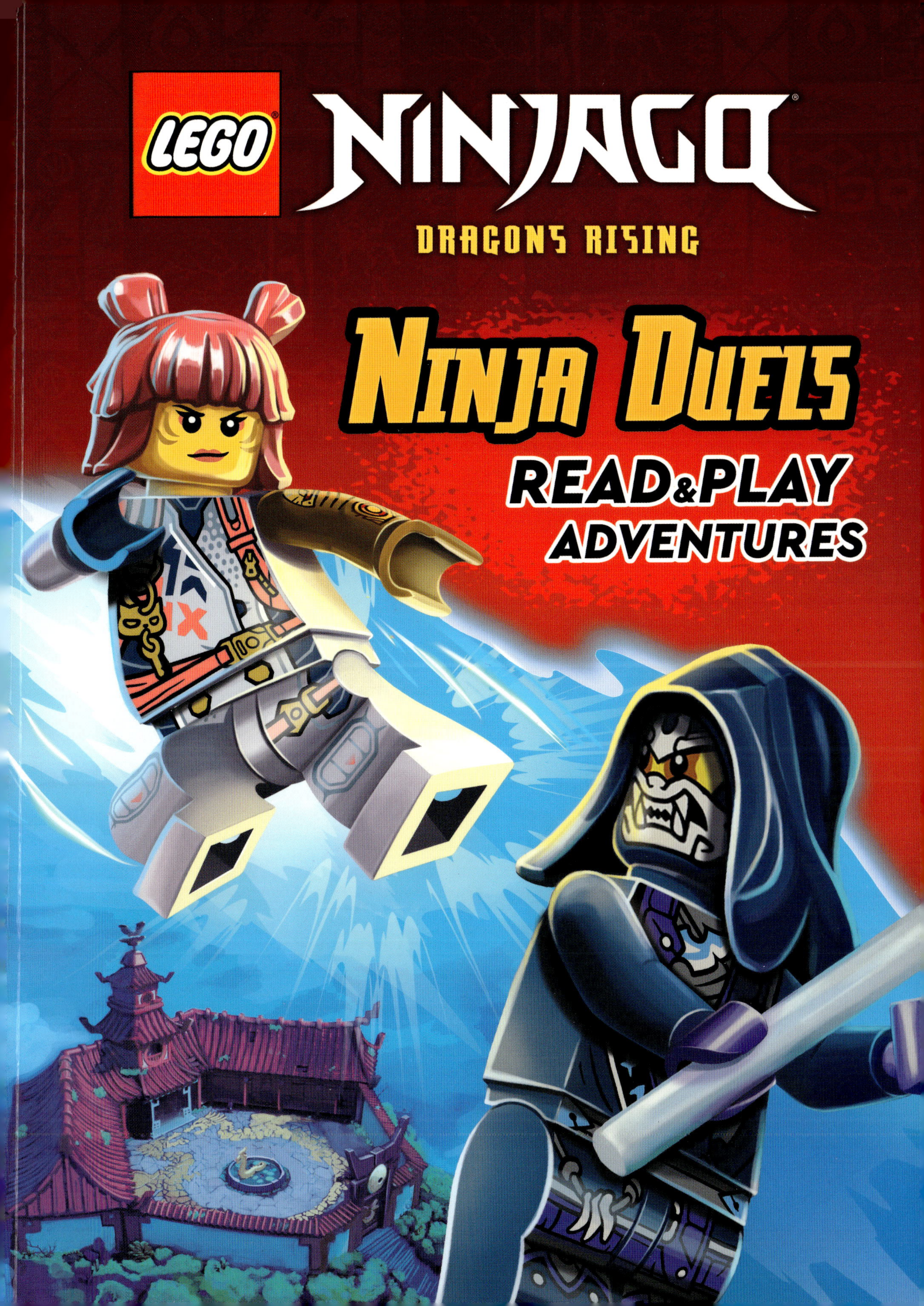
LEGO
NINJAGO
DRAGONS RISING
NINJA DUELS
READ&PLAY
ADVENTURES

4 Read the stories on pages 18–25 (*Midnight Duel*) and 46–53 (*Dark Hoods Arena*).

5 Use the instructions on pages 14-17 and 42-45 to build the mini builds. Both stories feature one mini build and a rebuild for maximum ninja play.

6 Use the minifigures, mini builds, and scenes to play out your stories.

7 Read the trivia and complete the activities, challenges, and puzzles.

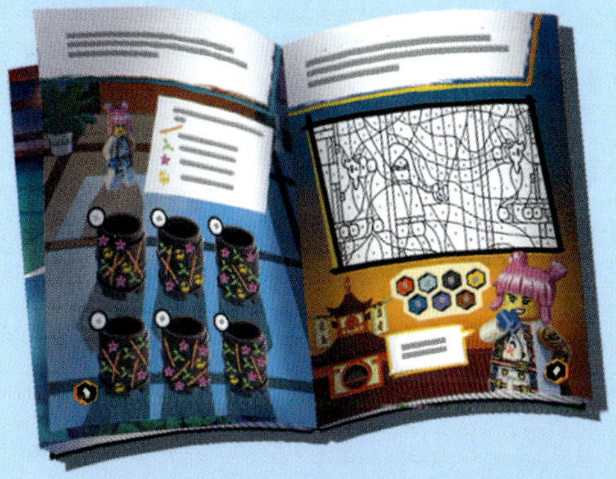

SORA

Sora has always been obsessed with technology! But her adventure with science truly began when she was still living in Imperium. Her dragon friend, Riyu, is helping her unlock her potential—the power to control technology! Join Sora and her friends in the fight against fearsome foes, especially the Wolf Mask Warrior.

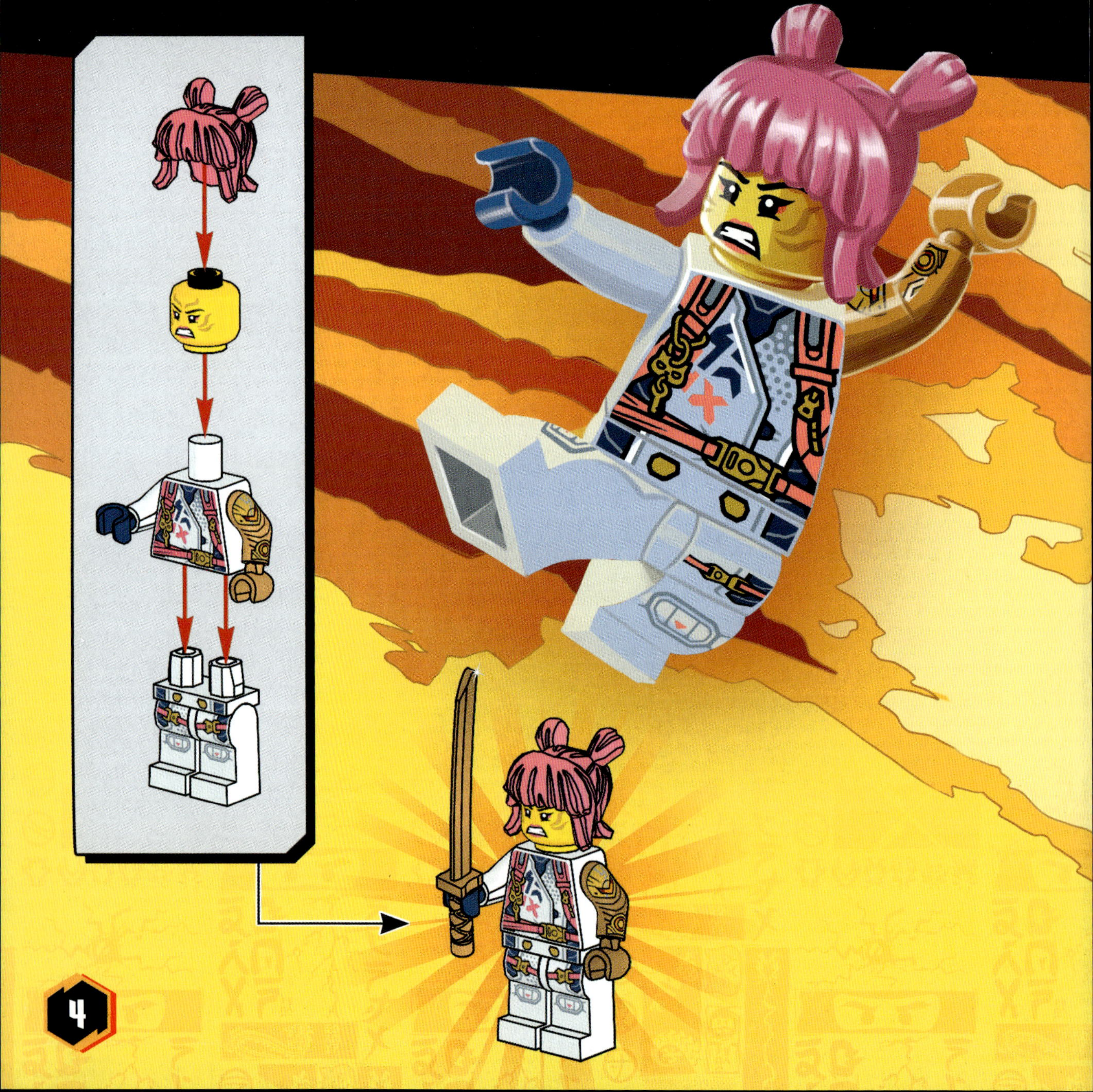

Wolf Mask Warrior

Like all warriors from Lord Ras's new Wolf Mask Army, this one is a powerful and highly skilled fighter. He is a trained spy and stealth attacker who is eager to take on any opponent. His mission is to find the new ninja and their young dragon—and then bring them to Lord Ras!

Build the Play Scenes

1 First, prepare the bricks you'll need to connect the elements of the set.

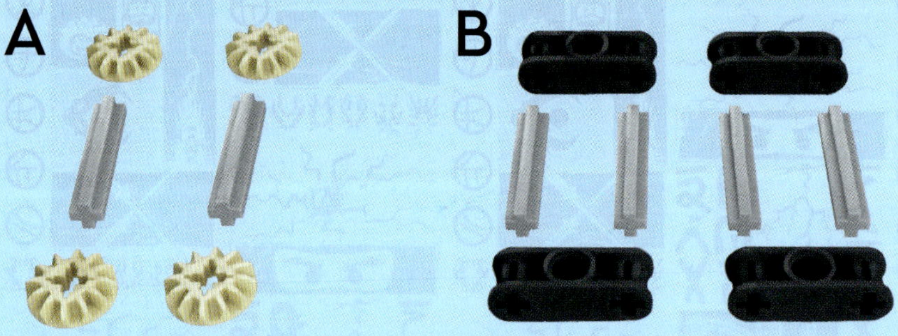

2 Then, open the box and turn it upside down.

3 Next, turn the wrap inside out. Fold it and use the bricks shown in Step 1A to fasten the top corners of the scene together.

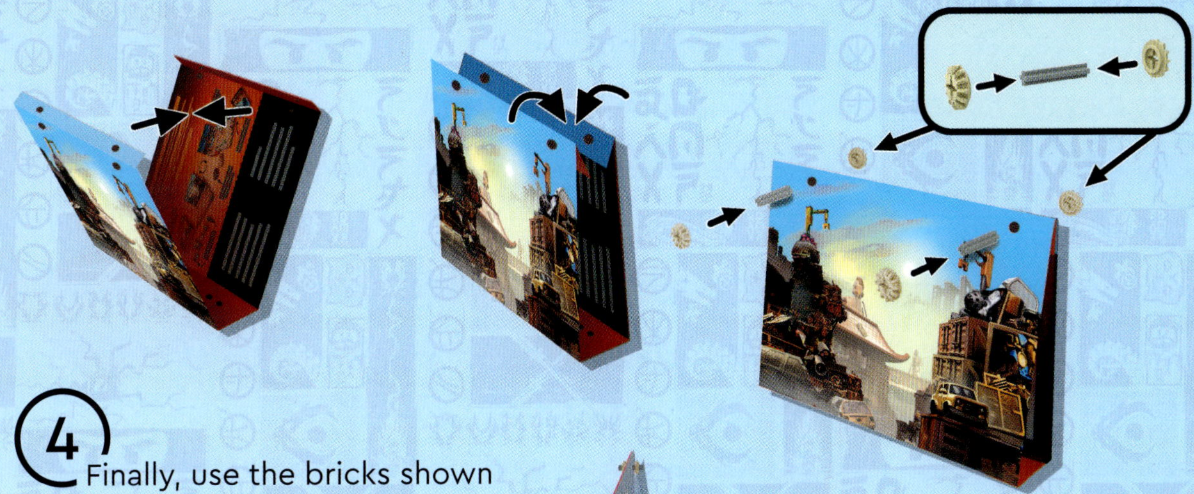

4 Finally, use the bricks shown in Step 1B to fasten the play scene to the box.

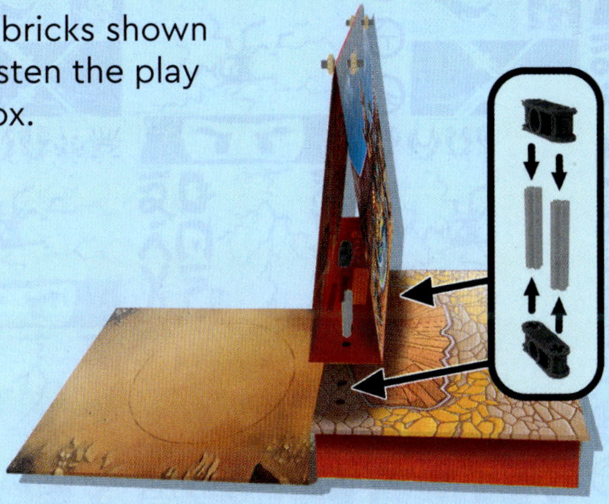

5 Add the brick boxes and platform to complete the play scene. Now you're ready to play out ninja duels!

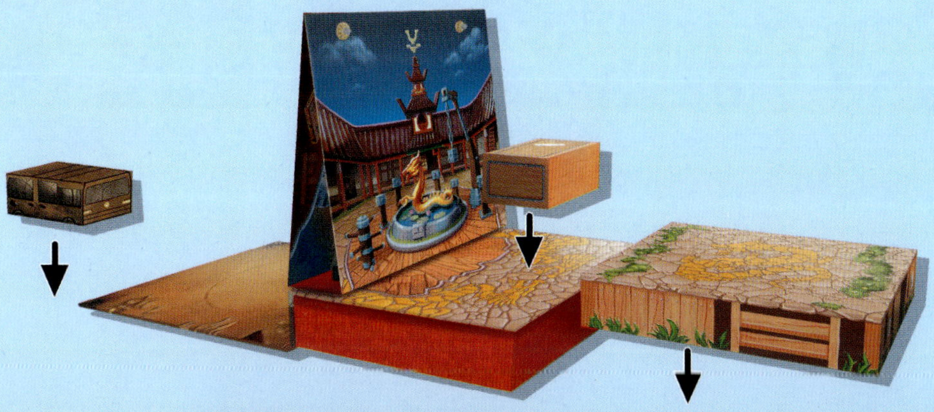

NEW MENACE TO THE MERGED WORLD

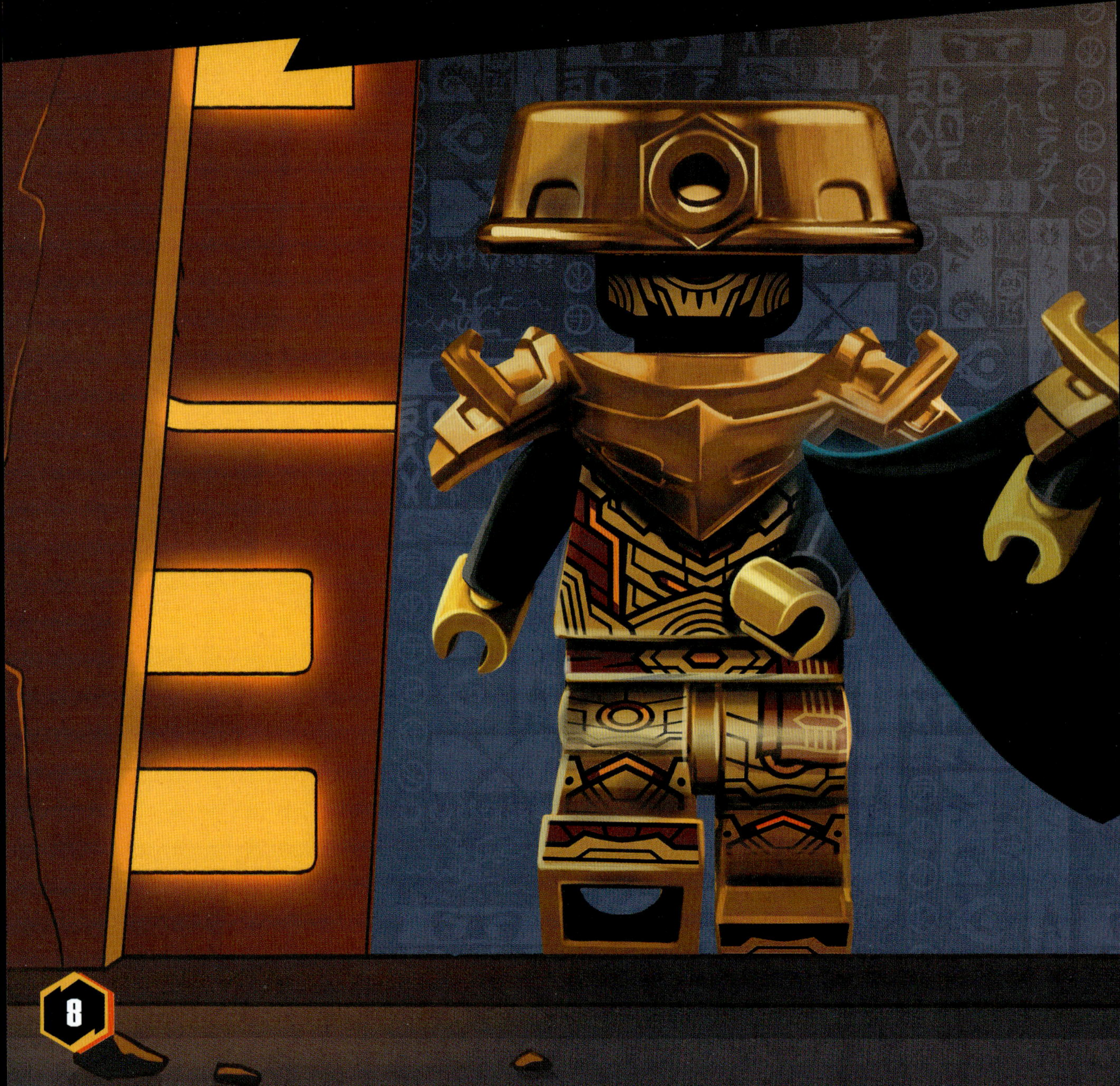

The Merge caused Ninjago's parallel realms to become one planet full of adventure, power, mystery, and, best of all, dragons. It so happens that dragons are extremely important to Imperium, one of the new realms in the post-Merge world. Empress Beatrix and her minions will stop at nothing to track dragons in each realm and capture them . . .

Where are the Ninja?

The Merge caused chaos in the world of Ninjago and the realms that joined it. The ninja were separated and, after a long time searching for each other, were partially reunited. They also found new members: Sora, Arin, and baby dragon, Riyu.

The ninja are trying to understand the effects of the Merge. They travel to many new places to learn the truth and stave off danger.

New enemies, called the Imperium Claws, hunt dragons across the united realms. The ninja do their best to protect the majestic creatures.

During the Merge, sources of Elemental Energy surged across the United Realms, awakening new Elemental Powers in Sora and other citizens.

Imperium

The super modern Imperium owes its advanced technology and comfortable lifestyle to... dragons. Imperium's scientists use the energy drained from captured dragons to fuel the growth of their kingdom.

Empress Beatrix is proud of her perfect kingdom. She wants to build an invincible army and conquer the newly-merged realms.

Imperium's dragon hunters and their modern drones roam all the realms. No dragon is safe anymore.

The powerful Lord Ras serves the Empress. But when an opportunity arises, he creates his own army to follow his own secret plans.

Wolf Mask Warriors are loyal to Lord Ras. These skilled warriors are prepared to follow every order of their ruthless commander.

Build the Practice Dummy

Build a practice dummy for Sora. Use it to help her train in the Monastery of Spinjitzu.

1

2

3

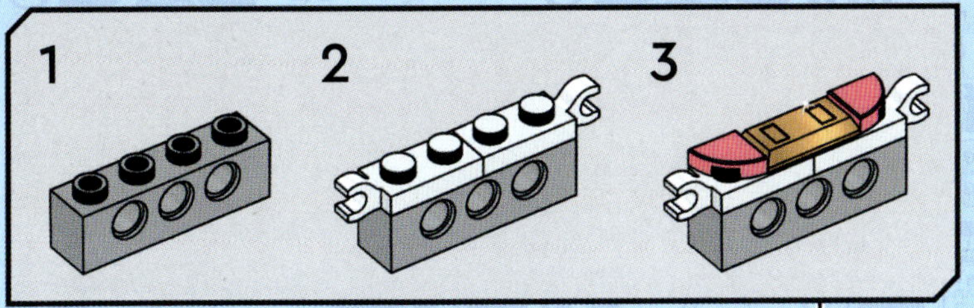

4

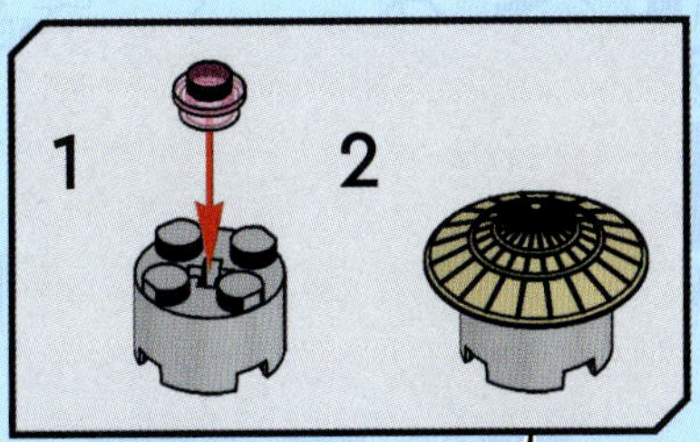

5

6

Build the Flying Combat Drone

Rebuild the practice dummy into a flying combat drone and continue Sora's training!

1

2

3

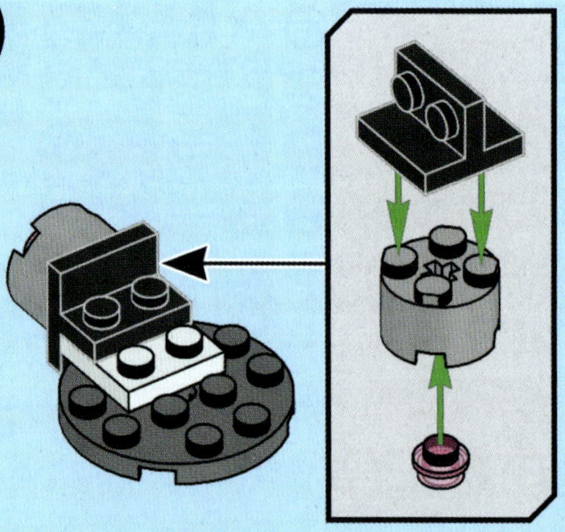

4

5

6

7

Midnight Duel

Night fell over the Monastery of Spinjitzu and the moon shone on the stately building.

Suddenly, a shadow flashed over the monastery and silently landed on the roof.

At the exact same time, Sora opened her eyes. She rose with alarm and looked around. Something wasn't right!

She stepped into the hallway and looked through the window. It seemed as if the whole world was asleep. Sora took a deep breath and walked along the hallway. Besides herself, only Lloyd,

Arin, and the little dragon Riyu were in the monastery tonight. She peeked into the room where Arin and Riyu were sleeping. One of them was snoring loudly, like a freight train. She couldn't make out who it was.

Then, out of the corner of her eye, she saw something move quickly outside the window.

"Who's there?" Sora called out. "Is that you, Lloyd?"

There was no answer. Alert and listening for any unusual sounds, Sora went downstairs. She was sure that a stranger was in the building.

Sora knew that she had to protect Riyu, whose presence in the monastery must have attracted an Imperium spy. The only way to do this was to divert the enemy's attention to herself.

She walked into the kitchen as if nothing had happened and sipped some water. Then she headed toward the dojo. She sensed that the intruder followed her.

The dojo has only one entrance and no windows, she thought. *A perfect spot for a trap!*

Sora walked into the dark room and grabbed a sword. Pretending it was her night practice, she started hitting an armed dummy. The dummy spun dangerously with each blow.

Suddenly, Sora jumped up, did a somersault in the air, landed next to the door, and quickly flipped on the light switch. The

intruder, a Wolf Mask Warrior, stood right in front of her, blinded be the light!

"Gotcha!" Sora said. "You're after Riyu, right?"

Without a word, the Wolf Mask Warrior whirled his spear so fast that it blurred. He wasn't in the mood for talking, apparently.

"Lloyd can do that a thousand times faster," Sora shouted and rushed toward him.

The Wolf Mask Warrior smoothly dodged her blows, jumping from place to place like a shadow.

Suddenly, he attacked. The head of his spear flashed in the light like a flickering flame. Now Sora backed away.

Then she pounced on him, but the warrior blocked her blows and knocked the sword out of her hand. He was a good fighter!

But Sora was trained by Lloyd, the legendary Green Ninja. She jumped into the air again, landed behind the practice dummy, and kicked it hard to make it spin. The Wolf Mask Warrior, who was rushing toward Sora, was caught by surprise. The dummy's heavy arm hit him and sent him sprawling on the floor.

Sora knew she didn't have much time before her opponent got up on his feet to attack her again. She had a plan, but she had to hurry. A bit nervous, her hands shaking, Sora turned to the dummy . . .

Meanwhile, the Wolf Mask Warrior groaned and shook his head, trying to see through the stars that swirled before his eyes.

As he started to see more clearly, he realized that these stars were actually parts of the dummy that were flying through the air. Clicking, connecting, and turning, these parts formed into something completely new–a drone.

Sora grabbed her sword and hopped onto the newly created drone. Armed with two additional swords, she circled the dojo, as if on a hoverboard, and then she struck from the air. Turning somersaults, the Wolf Mask Warrior fought back, but he didn't stand a chance. After taking Sora's blows, he fell to the floor, exhausted.

Suddenly, Arin and Riyu ran into the dojo. "Who? What? How?" Arin stammered sleepily.

But before Sora replied, Lloyd also rushed in. "Pack you gear, we have to go! The team needs us!" he exclaimed. "Say goodbye to your masked sparring partner, Sora."

Sora looked at the miserable Wolf Mask Warrior. "Hold on to the drone, buddy," she said. "You're going out!".

***

Sometime later, the Wolf Mask Warrior found himself sitting on the ground far from the monastery. He still felt dizzy from the fast ride that Sora had given him.

On the grass next to him, he saw a cookie wrapped in a piece of paper with something written on it. The note said:

Hey! It was a close fight, but you lost. Work out more before we face off again! Enjoy your little consolation prize!

The Wolf Mask Warrior sighed. The ninja and the dragon were gone. His mission was a disaster. He knew Lord Ras would not be happy . . .

At least the cookie was delicious!

THE END

Help Sora find the spy! The Wolf Mask Warrior is hiding in one of these barrels. Use the hints below to find him.

THE BARREL IS DECORATED WITH:

- more than three swords
- fewer than three dragons
- more than three flowers
- one Master Wu

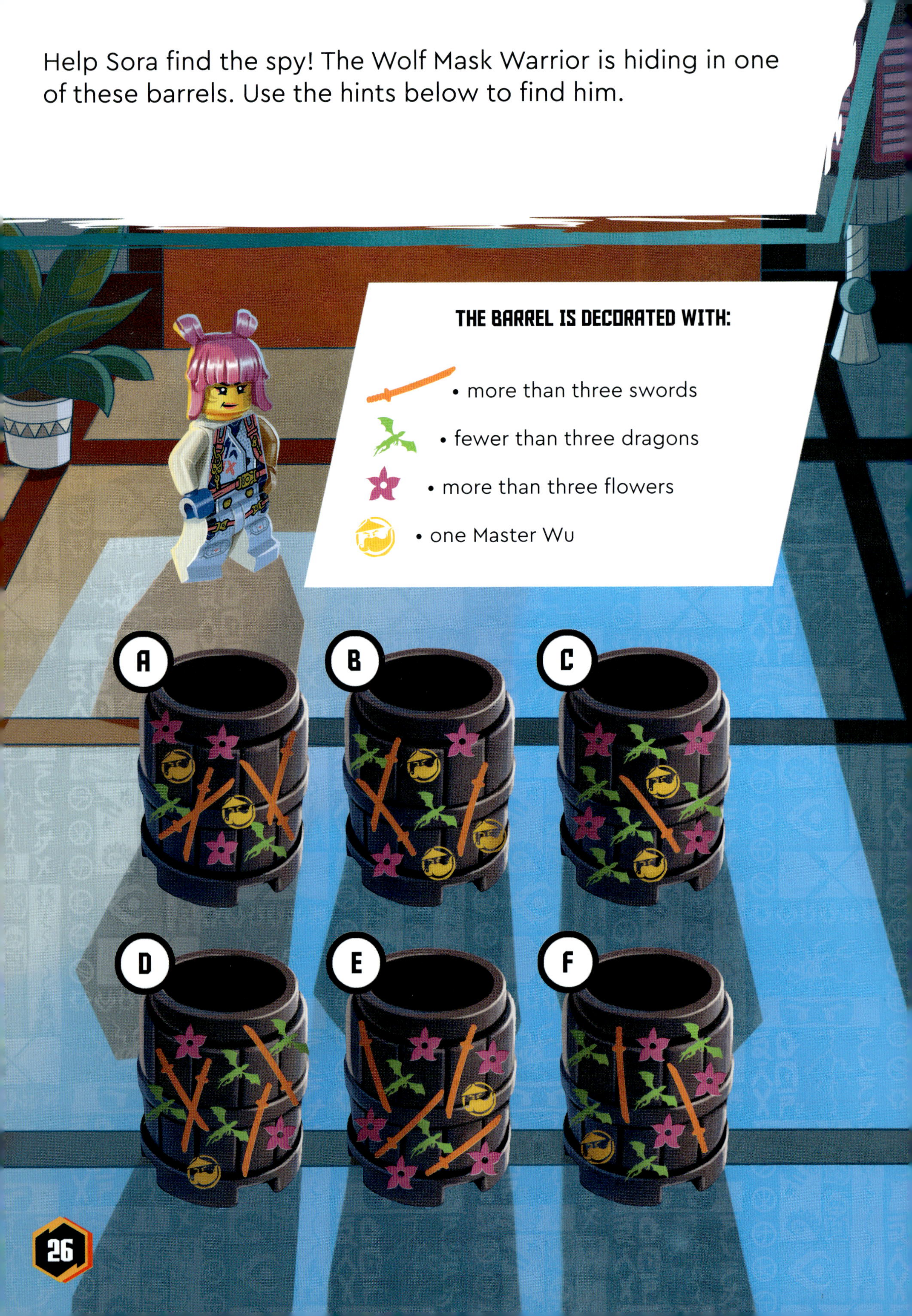

The Wolf Mask Warrior thinks he's a master of disguise! Help Sora find the spy by using the code to color the picture below.

Sora is ready to fight the Wolf Mask Warrior, but she doesn't have a weapon! Use your technology skills to help her. Grab a pencil and create awesome weapons and vehicles for her to use in battle.

LET'S SEE WHO'LL BE THE FIRST TO RUN!

Sora is tracking the Wolf Mask Warrior. Help her find him by circling his matching shadow.

Sora is close to capturing the Wolf Mask Warrior! Can you help her find the path through the temple so she can finally catch him?

Sora has finally found the Wolf Mask Warrior in an abandoned room. But, when she turns on the light, the spy jumps from fright. Can you draw what scared him?

Will the chase never end? The spy is now hiding in a tightly locked room. Help Sora crack the code to open the door. Punch in the numbers by following the arrows in the box.

Sora is rebuilding a training dummy to turn it into a combat drone, but a few bricks are missing! Find the missing bricks shown in the white oval and circle them.

Each of the small pictures below contains one item that doesn't match the large picture of the Wolf Mask Warrior. Circle the item that doesn't match in each small picture.

LIFE AFTER IMPERIUM

Empress Beatrix's sinister plans to conquer the merged world have been overthrown! The ninja have defeated the Empress and her forces in an epic battle in the streets of Imperium. Lord Ras has vanished without a trace, and dragons are no longer hunted by the Imperium Claws. However, for the protectors of the merged world, it is not yet time to rest . . .

THE CROSSROADS

The world of Ninjago and the other once-separate realms now exist as continents sharing the same sky and Endless Sea. The Crossroads, a neighborhood on the outskirts of Ninjago City, is a place where people from different places have learned to live together in harmony . . .

The residents of the Crossroads are a lively and diverse community. The Crossroads Carnival is a joyful celebration of their similarities and differences.

The mech race, held every Friday, is a big sporting event that connects the Crossroads community. Sora and Arin never miss the chance to participate in it!

Having defeated Imperium, the ninja now work together to protect the world—and the Crossroads—from everyday threats.

Great Power on the Rise

When Sora was growing up in Imperium, she thought she would become one of the kingdom's best scientists. But, when the young inventor looked for a fresh start in the Crossroads, she discovered that destiny had chosen an unexpected path for her . . .

Thanks to Lloyd's guidance and training, Sora has learned ninja skills and unlocked her potential as the powerful Master of Technology!

Lloyd is amazed by the uniqueness of Sora's power. He believes that someday Sora may become one of the greatest Elemental Masters!

The merged world will soon need another mighty protector like Sora, since a new menace is already emerging from the shadows . . .

Build the Jet Pack

Build a jet pack for Sora that she can use to duel in the arena.

1

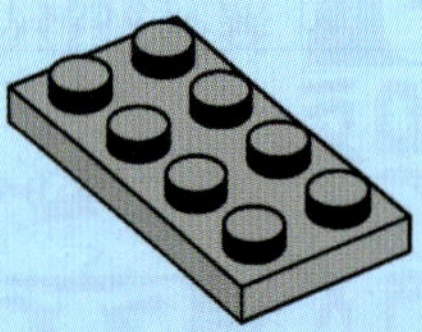

2

3

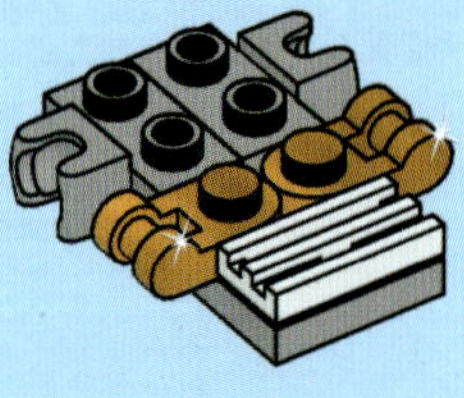

4

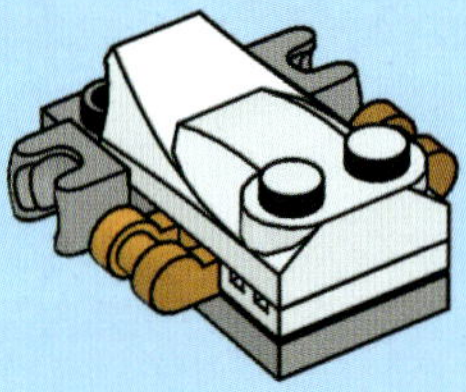

5

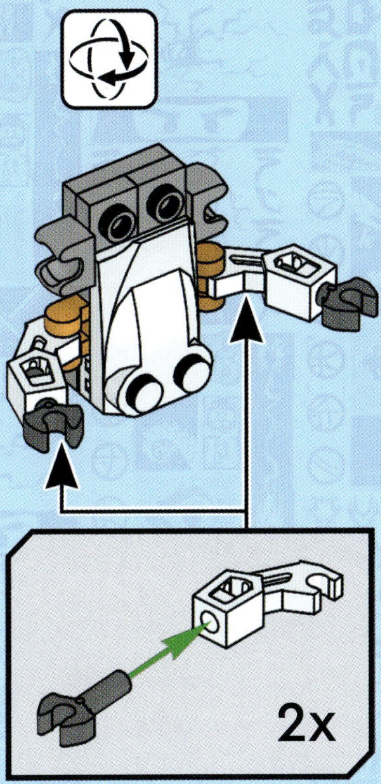

6

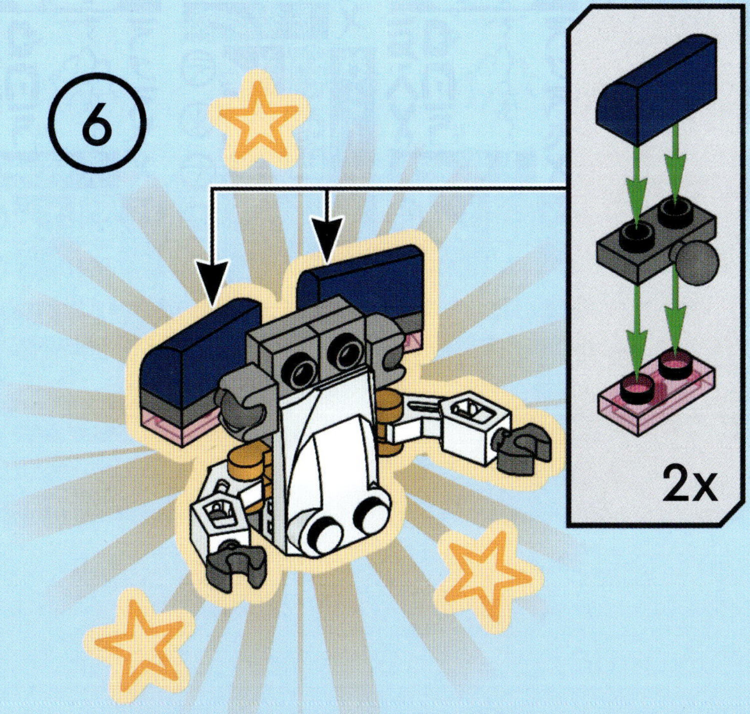

Build the Combat Mech

Rebuild the jet pack into a combat mech and continue Sora's duel.

1

2

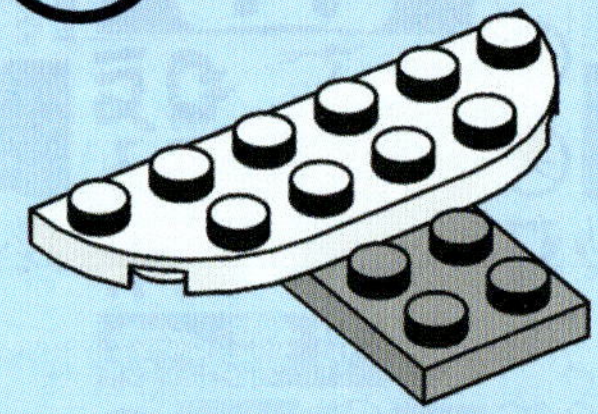

3

4

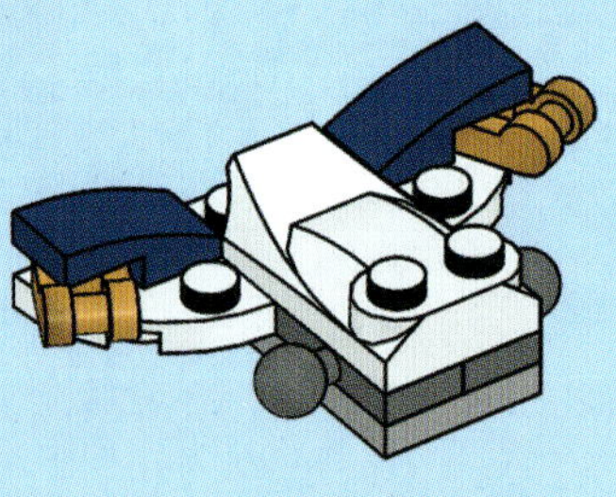

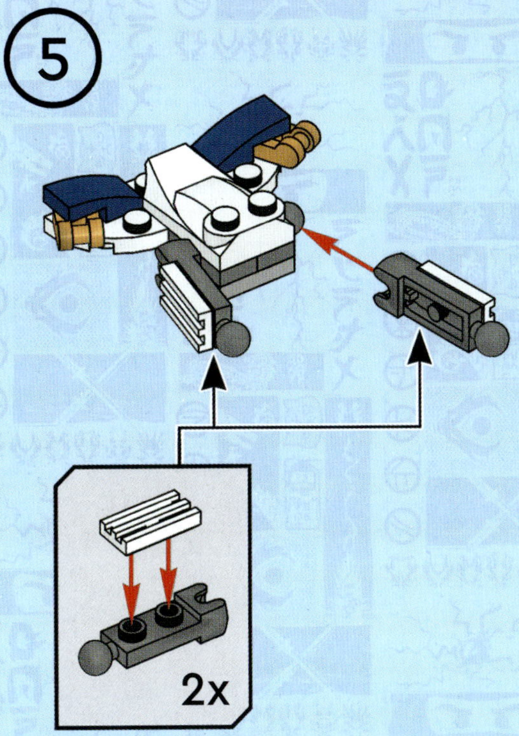
5
2x

6
1
2
2x

7
2x

Dark Hoods Arena

The evening was noisy and full of lights. Nothing surprising—after all, it was the Crossroads. Neon signs illuminated the neighborhood where crowds were gathering in the narrow streets full of shops and restaurants. Sora sped up and the jet pack carried her skywards.

She was searching the Crossroads with Arin and Riyu, trying to find any trace of the mysterious thief who had recently been breaking into antique shops, but not stealing anything.

Still, the thief must've been looking for something among the ancient books and rare artifacts. That was worrying.

So far, the search had been fruitless. So the group decided to split up. Arin searched the streets with Riyu, while Sora patrolled the city from the air.

She spotted an enormous junkyard and flew down to examine it when, suddenly, a shuriken whirred through the darkness and hit her jet pack. Startled, Sora jerked the controls, which caused her to start spinning rapidly. Before she knew it, she hit a wall, then she fell to the ground . . .

***

Sora lifted her head. She realized that she was lying among broken-down machines. Three hooded figures stood in front of her.

Sora jumped to her feet, prepared to fight. She heard whispers around her. She looked around—there were more people hidden in the darkness! Fighting was not an option.

One of the hooded figures stepped into the light. "It's the Dark Hoods territory," said a stern female voice. "You're trespassing!"

"I'm not looking for any trouble," Sora assured.

"We don't like intruders," said the woman. "But we protect the lost... What is it that you're looking for, then?"

"Um... A thief," Sora answered.

"That's what the boy said," whispered a figure in the shadow.

"The boy?" Sora gulped. She had a bad feeling.

"Yes," said the woman. "We caught him and his dragon trespassing, too."

Uh-oh! Looks like Arin and Riyu are in trouble, Sora thought. "They're with me! They must leave with me!" she said.

"That's what the masked warrior said," another shadow whispered.

The masked warrior? Sora thought. *Could it be Lloyd?*

"We caught him too," said the woman. "He was—"

"Trespassing!" finished the figures in the shadow.

The hooded woman leaned toward Sora and looked her in the eyes. "It's not wise to trust strangers. You and the masked warrior say the same thing. Coincidence? I don't think so. One of you must be lying. Prepare to confront your rival!"

***

Ten minutes later, Sora was standing in the middle of the junkyard, in a small arena, surrounded by hooded figures. Suddenly, someone appeared on the other side of the ring. Sora recognized him as soon as he stepped into the light.

It wasn't Lloyd. It was the Wolf Mask Warrior!

It was clear he had been following Arin and Riyu before they fell into the hands of the Dark Hoods.

"So we meet again," Sora said. "Did you remember to work out more after our last face off?"

The Wolf Mask Warrior only grumbled in response. Then he flashed his razor-sharp claws and took a fearsome combat stance.

Sora was not going to waste time waiting for his attack. She started her jet pack and charged at her opponent first. But the Wolf Mask Warrior suddenly dodged her, and the girl flew past him.

"Whoa! So you did practice," Sora said.

The Wolf Mask Warrior reached out for his spear and threw it at her. The weapon hit Sora's jet pack, which immediately released a trail of dark smoke and stalled. Sora landed hard on the arena floor.

The Warrior laughed and jumped at his opponent, swiping the broken jet pack off her back with one quick move.

This doesn't look good, Sora thought. *I know what to do!*

The Warrior attacked again, but Sora dodged his blows. In order to move away from him, Sora did a somersault and landed next to the jet pack.

"I have practiced too, you know," she said, looking the Wolf Mask Warrior straight in the eye. She pulled out her hands and a purple glow lit up the broken jet pack. The device fell into pieces that started to float and swirl above the arena.

The Wolf Mask Warrior and the hooded spectators were awestruck. They watched in silence as the bricks quickly reassembled into something new. When the last element fell into place, in the middle of the arena stood a mighty combat mech.

Sora quickly jumped into the mech and charged at the Wolf Mask Warrior. Now she had a clear advantage. The Warrior tried to defend himself with his sharp claws, but soon he was lying on the ground, defeated. Sora tore off a piece of the rope hanging over the arena and used it to tie up her opponent. She even created a cute bow on top of his head!

The mech swung its sword menacingly. Sora turned to the Dark Hoods.

"Can I see my friends now?" she asked.

***

The morning sun was already shining in the Crossroads when two young ninja, a baby dragon, and three hooded figures reached the limits of the Dark Hoods territory.

"I'm really glad you're both fine," said Sora, looking at Arin and Riyu. "But I didn't hear any of you actually thanking me for rescuing you!"

Arin looked at her, surprised. "Rescuing us? I didn't know we were in danger! They gave us pillows and blankets, we had a nice nap, then we had some snacks . . ."

With an astonished expression on her face, Sora turned to look at their hooded companions.

"I told you that we protect the lost," the Dark Hoods leader explained.

"Then why did you have me fight that Warrior?" Sora asked.

"Um . . . We didn't," the woman said. "We wanted you to confront him. Then we planned to take you both to see your friends. They would've known who to trust, right?"

"Right!" Arin said. Riyu just nodded.

The woman leaned over to Sora and whispered, "Look after these two!"

"I definitely will," assured Sora.

THE END

Can you help Sora find Arin? Locate the START octagon below. Then, follow the arrow and move up two octagons. Continue to follow the arrows and move the number of spaces noted in each octagon you land upon until you reach Arin!

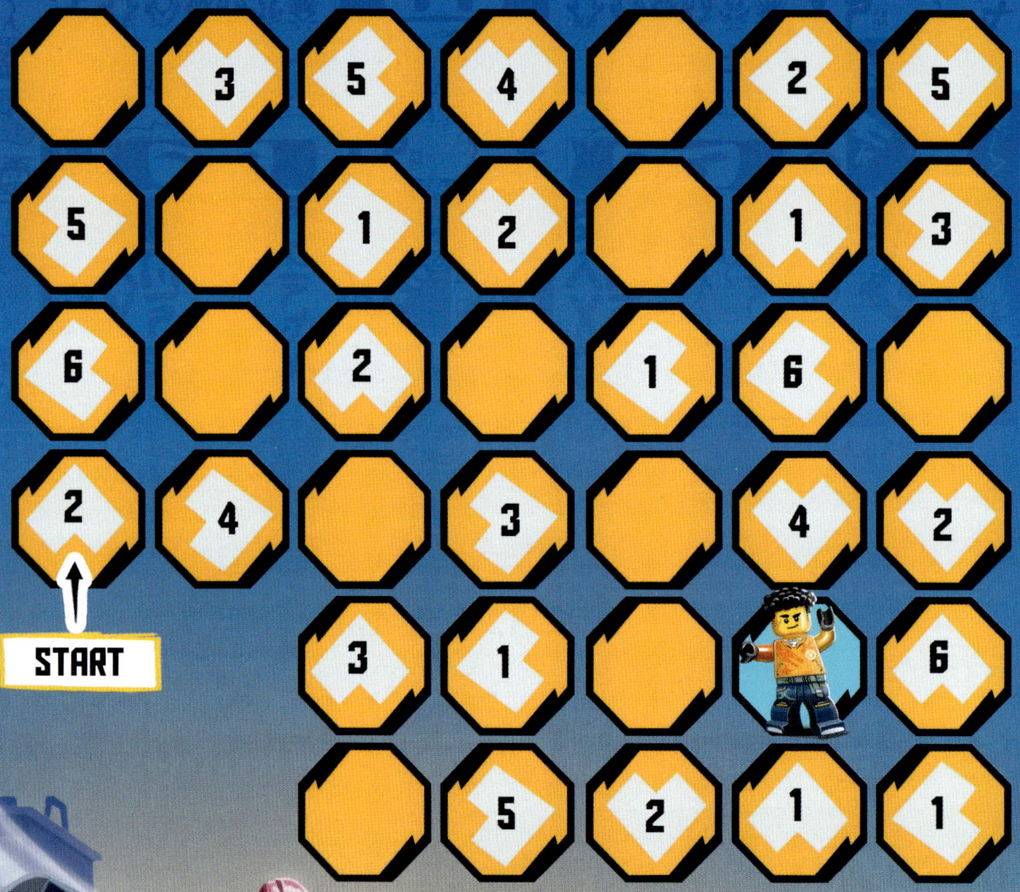

Sora needs to be careful exploring this dangerous junkyard. Help her find six Whack Rats hiding among the junk.

The Dark Hoods have captured Arin. Which junk heap is guarded by more warriors? Find it and help Sora save Arin.

What would Sora build if she couldn't transform her jet pack into a mech? Draw it below and list its powers!

Sora is in a fierce fight with the Wolf Mask Warrior. Can you accept the challenge to find ten differences between the two pictures before the duel is over?

Sora delivers a final blow! Help her find the missing piece she needs to complete her picture.

Sora is practicing combat moves in her mech. Find the two stances that match and draw a line to connect them.

It's time to end this fight once and for all! Untangle the lines to help Sora find her mech.

Who is hiding below? Connect the dots to find out!

Answers

p. 26

E

p. 27

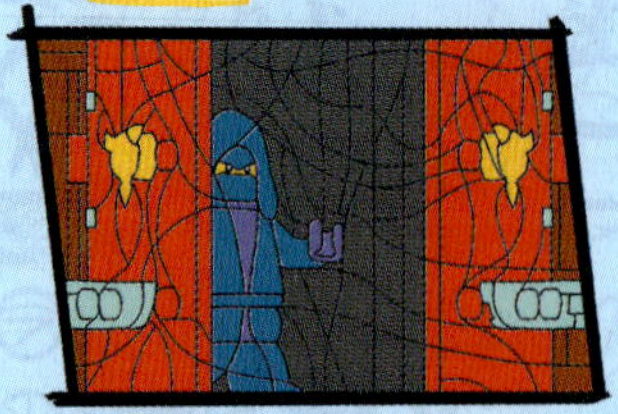

p. 30

D

p. 31

p. 33

41236523

p. 34

p. 35

p. 54

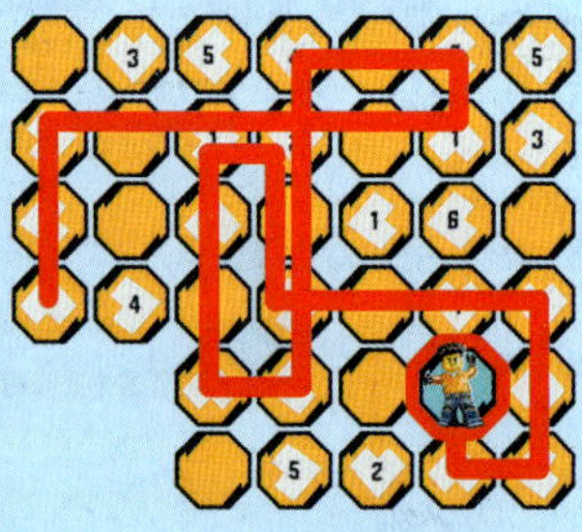

p. 55

p. 56

pp. 58–59

p. 60

D

p. 61

B

G

p. 62

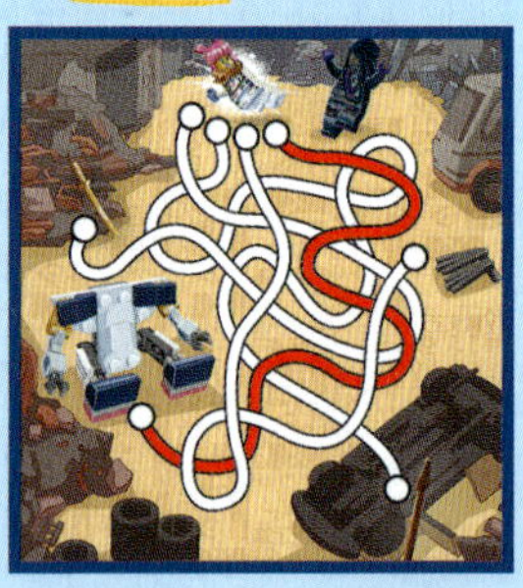

p. 63

Build your own LEGO® NINJAGO® minifigures and get ready for an epic battle between Sora and the Wolf Mask Warrior!

AMEET Manufactured by AMEET Sp. z o.o. under license from the LEGO Group.

AMEET Sp. z o.o.
Nowe Sady 6, 94-102 Łódź – Poland
ameet@ameet.eu
www.ameet.eu

Published in the US and Canada by Sourcebooks
1935 Brookdale Road, Suite 139
Naperville, IL 60563
Please keep the Sourcebooks address for future reference.
www.LEGO.com

LEGO BOOKS

Manufactured, printed, and assembled in Heshan, China.

sourcebooks **wonderland**
sourcebookskids.com

This book is part of a set.

6+

FSC www.fsc.org MIX Supporting responsible forestry FSC® C144528